Dragon's Snowy Day

Adapted by Sonia Sander

ISBN 0-439-80163-X

© 2005 Cité-Amérique – scopas medien AG – Image Plus.
DRAGON™ is a property of Cité-Amérique – scopas medien AG – Image Plus.
Used under license by Scholastic Inc. All rights reserved.
Published by Scholastic Inc. SCHOLASTIC and associated logos are trademarks and/or registered trademarks of Scholastic Inc.

12 11 10 9 8 7 6 5 4 3 2 1   5 6 7 8 9/0

Printed in the U.S.A.
First printing, December 2005

SCHOLASTIC INC.
New York   Toronto   London   Auckland   Sydney
Mexico City   New Delhi   Hong Kong   Buenos Aires

One day Dragon woke up
from a long, cozy sleep
to find snow everywhere.
Dragon loved a snowy day!

Dragon could not wait to
get outside. The first thing
he did was catch snowflakes
on his tongue. Dragon loved
the taste of snowflakes.

"I'm going to make the biggest snowman ever," Dragon said. The snowman was so big, it ran over Mailmouse! So Dragon made a smaller snowman.

Dragon liked his new smaller
snowman but it was still not
quite right. So Dragon turned
the snowman into a snowdragon.

Dragon had a great time playing
with his new snowdragon friend.

Then it was time to go
inside for lunch.

"I miss my snowdragon
friend," said Dragon.
Dragon had an idea.
He brought his snowdragon
inside the house.

But the snowdragon began to melt!
"It's too warm in the house for a
snowdragon," said Dragon.

Dragon gave his snowdragon
some ice cream to cool it down.
But the snowdragon kept melting.
It was not cold enough inside
Dragon's house.

Dragon opened the doors and
windows to let in the cold air.

Then he put out the fire.

It worked!

The snowdragon was
not melting anymore,
but Dragon was freezing!

"Hello!" called Mailmouse
from the front door.
"It's colder in here
than it is outside!"

Dragon decided to go outside to get warm. "Aren't you cold sitting out here?" asked Mailmouse.

"Yes," said Dragon.

"I am very cold."

"Why don't you go inside and warm up?" asked Mailmouse. "Then the snowdragon that is inside will melt," said Dragon. "Put your snowdragon out here in the snow where it won't melt," said Mailmouse.

Dragon thought that was a very good idea. He put his snowdragon back in the snow where it would be very cold.

Dragon shut all
the windows and doors.
Dragon sat by the fire
until he was nice
and warm again.

For the rest of the day,
Dragon played outside
with his snowdragon.
When he got too cold,
he went inside to warm
up by the fire.

Finally it was bedtime.
"Good night, Snowdragon,"
Dragon said from his window.
Then he crawled into his
toasty-warm bed
and fell fast asleep.